Beauty and the Beast

Retold by Susanna Davidson

Illustrated by John Joven

Reading consultant: Alison Kelly

There was once a poor man
named Pierre who had
three daughters.

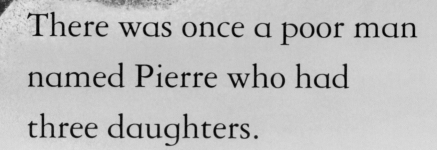

I hate being
poor.

Papa's so
hopeless.

The older daughters were
cruel and spiteful.

Only the youngest, Belle,
was kind to him.

One day, Pierre
decided to go to the
city, far away.

I can make
money in
the city.

"I'll bring you gifts," he
said. "What would you like?"

4

"Bring me jewels," said the
eldest daughter.

"Bring me fine dresses,"
said the second.

"Belle, what do you want?"
asked her father.

"Just your safe return,"
she replied.

"I'll bring you back a rose,
to match your beauty,"
he promised.

She should have asked for more.

Silly Belle!

Pierre reached the city safely. But on his return, he was caught in a terrible storm.

Lightning zig-zagged through the trees.

Drenched with rain, his teeth chattering, he knocked on the castle door.

It creaked open.

Inside, he found a table,
laden with food.

"Eat," said a deep voice.

Pierre looked around,
but no one was there.

Hungrily, he began to eat.

"Time for bed," said
the mysterious voice.
Pierre climbed the stairs.

At the top was a bedroom,
the bed freshly made.

Pierre slipped between the
sheets and fell fast asleep.

15

The next morning, the sun
shone once more.

Pierre wanted to say thank
you for the food and the bed...

...but the castle was empty.
In the garden, he found a
beautiful rose bush.

"For Belle," he thought,
picking a rose.

A moment later, he heard
a terrible ROAR.

Pierre turned and cried
out in shock. There stood
a hideous beast.

"How dare you steal from me?" the Beast snarled.

"I gave you food
and a bed."

"I'm so sorry," said Pierre.

Forgive me!

"Too late," said the Beast. "For this, you die!"

Pierre began to sob. "I was only taking the rose for my youngest daughter."

The flower reminded me of her beauty.

The Beast looked thoughtful. "I'll let you go home," he said.

"But only to say goodbye to your family. One of you must return to pay the price."

Pierre agreed. He arrived home, full of worry.

Only Belle noticed
something was wrong.

At last, their father told
them about the Beast.

"I'll go to him," said Belle.

She rode through the woods to his castle. "What would the beast be like?" she wondered.

26

He welcomed her in. "I am your servant," he said.

Go wherever you like in the castle.

He gave her the finest food to eat and beautiful clothes to wear.

Every night, over supper, they would talk...

Then one night, the Beast asked Belle to marry him.

I cannot.

"I'm so sorry," said Belle.
"I love you only as a friend."

From that night on, Belle dreamed of a handsome prince.

She spent her days
wandering the magical castle.

Time passed, as if in a dream. "I am happy here," she said. "But I miss my family."

"Please, let me go home to them. I promise I'll return."

"You have one week," said
the Beast. "Take these..."

*A magic mirror
to show you
the palace.*

*A ring to
bring you
back to me.*

"Twist the ring three times.
It will magic you here."

Pierre was overjoyed to
see his daughter again.

I can only
stay a week...

But her sisters were
full of jealousy.

"It's not fair she has such a pretty dress," they said. "And those jewels."

We want them!

"Let's trick her into staying here with us," they decided.

Kind Belle believed them.

A week passed, and she
didn't return to the Beast.

"I must go back to him,"
she said, once another
week had passed.

Belle longed to see the Beast again. She missed their talks.

She missed the sound of his voice.

Belle gazed into the mirror.
It shimmered into life.

There lay the beast by the
rose bush, his eyes shut.

His breathing was slow
and ragged.

She took the ring he'd given
her and twisted it three times.

In an instant, she was at his side. "Wake up!" she cried. "What happened to you?"

"You didn't return," replied the Beast, his voice weak.

It broke my heart.

Tears fell from Belle's eyes.
"I love you," she said.

As Belle's tears dropped onto
the Beast, the air around him
filled with tiny stars.

A moment later he
changed... into the prince
from her dreams.

"My curse is over!" cried the prince. "Long ago, a wicked fairy changed me into a beast."

"The spell could only be broken if I found true love."

"And you have," said Belle.

About the story

Beauty and the Beast is an old, old story.
It was first told around 4,000 years ago,
although the version we know today
was written by a French writer,
Gabrielle-Suzanne Barbot de Villeneuve,
and was first published in 1740.

Designed by Laura Nelson Norris
Series designer: Russell Punter
Series editor: Lesley Sims

This edition first published in 2019 by Usborne Publishing Ltd.,
Usborne House, 83-85 Saffron Hill, London EC1N 8RT, England.
www.usborne.com Copyright © 2019, 2018 Usborne Publishing Ltd.